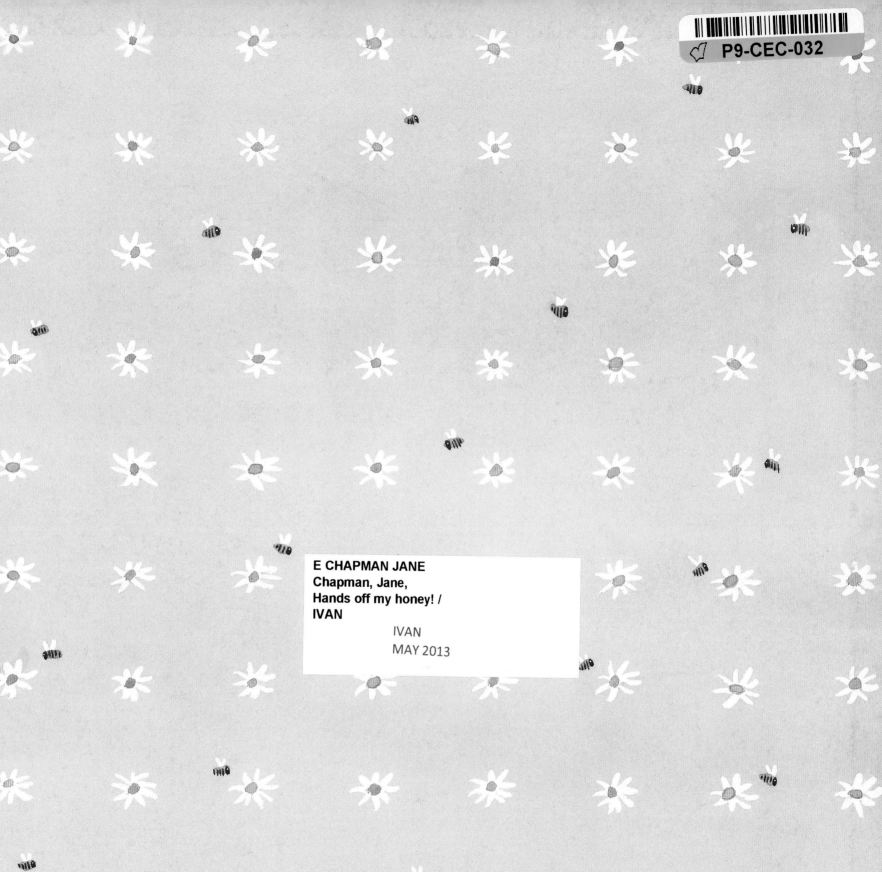

For Claire Warne, who shares
her shredder and computer
Thank you ~ JC & TW

tiger tales
an imprint of ME Media, LLC
5 River Road, Suite 128, Wilton, CT 06897
Published in the United States 2013
Originally published in Great Britain 2013
by Little Tiger Press
Text copyright © 2013 Jane Chapman
Illustrations copyright © 2013 Tim Warnes
CIP data is available
ISBN-13: 978-1-58925-142-7 • ISBN-10: 1-58925-142-3
Printed in China • LTP/1400/0497/1112

For more insight and activities,
visit us at www.tigertalesbooks.com

Hands off MY HONEY!

by Jane Chapman

Illustrated by Tim Warnes

tiger tales

Bear **stomped** and **stamped** to his hollow by the **big oak tree.**

The ground **rumbled**. The daisies **shook** and the leaves **trembled** in the trees.

"I have a **great big jar of delicious honey!**" Bear bellowed. "And it is **ALL mine!**"

Bear looked around, but everyone had disappeared.

"Don't even try to take a pawful!" he boomed. "I am the scariest bear in the forest and I won't share a single drop!"

HONE